The Answer

written by *Rebecca Sugar*

art by *Elle Michalka* and *Tiffany Ford*

CARTOON NETWORK BOOKS

An Imprint of Penguin Random House

For Ian, my Sapphire—RS

CARTOON NETWORK BOOKS
Penguin Young Readers Group
An Imprint of Penguin Random House LLC

STEVEN UNIVERSE, CARTOON NETWORK, the logos and all related characters and elements are trademarks of and © Cartoon Network. (s16). All rights reserved. Published in 2016 by Cartoon Network Books, an imprint of Penguin Random House LLC, 345 Hudson Street, New York, New York 10014. Manufactured in China.

ISBN 9780399541704   10 9 8 7 6 5 4 3 2 1

*T*his is the story
of Ruby and Sapphire's time
on the planet Earth.

This is the beginning of the story.

5,750 years ago,

the Earth was in the process of being conquered by Gems,

a space-faring race that always conquers planets,

because that's what Gems are supposed to do!

But a rebellious Rose Quartz burst out and said, "STOP!"

She liked the planet the way it was—
messy and pointless,
covered in ridiculous
plants and creatures
growing every which way
for no reason!

What could she like
about a planet like this?
Why would she fight
her fellow Gems?
And how could she be stopped?

The Gem with the answers
would be a Sapphire:
a rare Gem with the power
to see into the future.

This is the middle of the story.

And so a Sapphire came to Earth.

She was assigned three Ruby guards to protect her.
They were small, simple soldiers dispatched in groups,
so when the going got tough,
they could FUSE into ONE BIG RUBY!

Oh, hey—it's you! Hey! And there's me!

If you don't like stories that are scary and sad, you might want to stop reading here.

pphire knew that very soon, the
els would attack, and her Rubies
uld fuse, and would be defeated,

and only one would be left
helplessly watch while Sapphire
under the sword of a rebel Gem.

Huh? WHAT?

But that was what was supposed to happen,
so Sapphire didn't mind.

Sapphire had already accepted everything
that would ever happen to her.
She could see it ahead of her as easily as you
can flip to the end of this book.

The rebels would be caught, and punished,
and the colony would be completed just as planned.
And Sapphire would be taken back to
the Gem Homeworld, where she would come to.

And she would never see Earth or her Ruby guards again.

I don't know what to say. This doesn't happen!

Sapphire didn't have an answer! Ruby jumped to Sapphire's defense. The Gems turned all their anger toward Ruby.

You will be broken for this!

Wait! Leave her alone! This is MY fault.

They found themselves
alone together
on the surface of Earth.

What had Ruby done?
How could she call herself a Ruby?!
She was supposed to PROTECT Sapphire,
not strand her on a wild alien planet!

But as the sun rose over the hills,
their thoughts turned to each other,
and the impossible new Gem
they had created together.

Sapphire had never fused, she was never meant to!
She was never supposed to see dusk or dawn on Earth,
or find cold drops of water on young plants in the morning.

She was never meant to hear Ruby's laugh,
or watch her charge ahead
as if they both weren't lost!

Could this Gem's unthinkable
courage override reality?

Ruby had always fused!
She was always supposed to fuse
with other Rubies into BIGGER Rubies!
Never with anyone else,
and of course not with a Sapphire!

How could Ruby
have ever hoped to combine
with a Gem so valuable,
so precious, so powerful,
that she could see beyond
space and time?

Yeah, you're right!

Hey, let's go down there. Jump with me!

She was never meant to see Sapphire
look at her like this—
fascinated, bewildered, impressed—
as if Ruby were the most important
Gem in the universe!

What on Earth?!

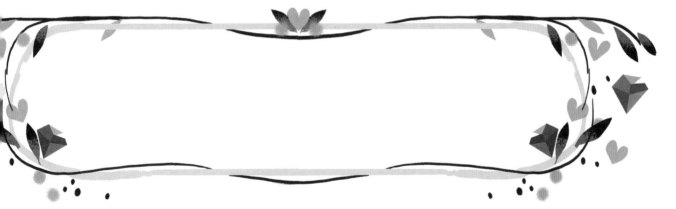

But neither of them could deny that these things
that were never supposed to happen were definitely happening!

And they started to wonder if what they were supposed to be
and everything they were supposed to do

might just have been one of
an infinite number of possibilities.

And what if Gems don't actually know what it means
to be a Ruby or a Sapphire,

if a Ruby can be special, and a Sapphire can be wrong?

What if no one can actually say for sure
that anything is meant to be anything,
and we're all supposed to figure it out in real time?

. . . or NOT!

Wow, it feels so different down here!

Yeah, I guess I never noticed it before.

Maybe it was just this planet,
and all its ridiculous plants and creatures
growing every which way for no reason,
that made certainty seem like foolishness,
and confusion start to make sense!

Ruby and Sapphire wondered if they'd get
an even clearer view of this incredible planet . . .

. . . if they tried looking at it through the eyes
of the Gem they'd made together!

And why not, when no one was watching?

Hey, I'm really sorry I ruined your story.

I like this version better! I didn't know we could just . . . change it to whatever we wanted.

Except . . . someone was!

It was the leader of the rebellion, Rose Quartz.

Ruby and Sapphire's Fusion was scared at first, but Rose Quartz stood in awe of their discovery.

She wanted to meet this Gem who shouldn't exist. She wanted to hear this story's secret ending.